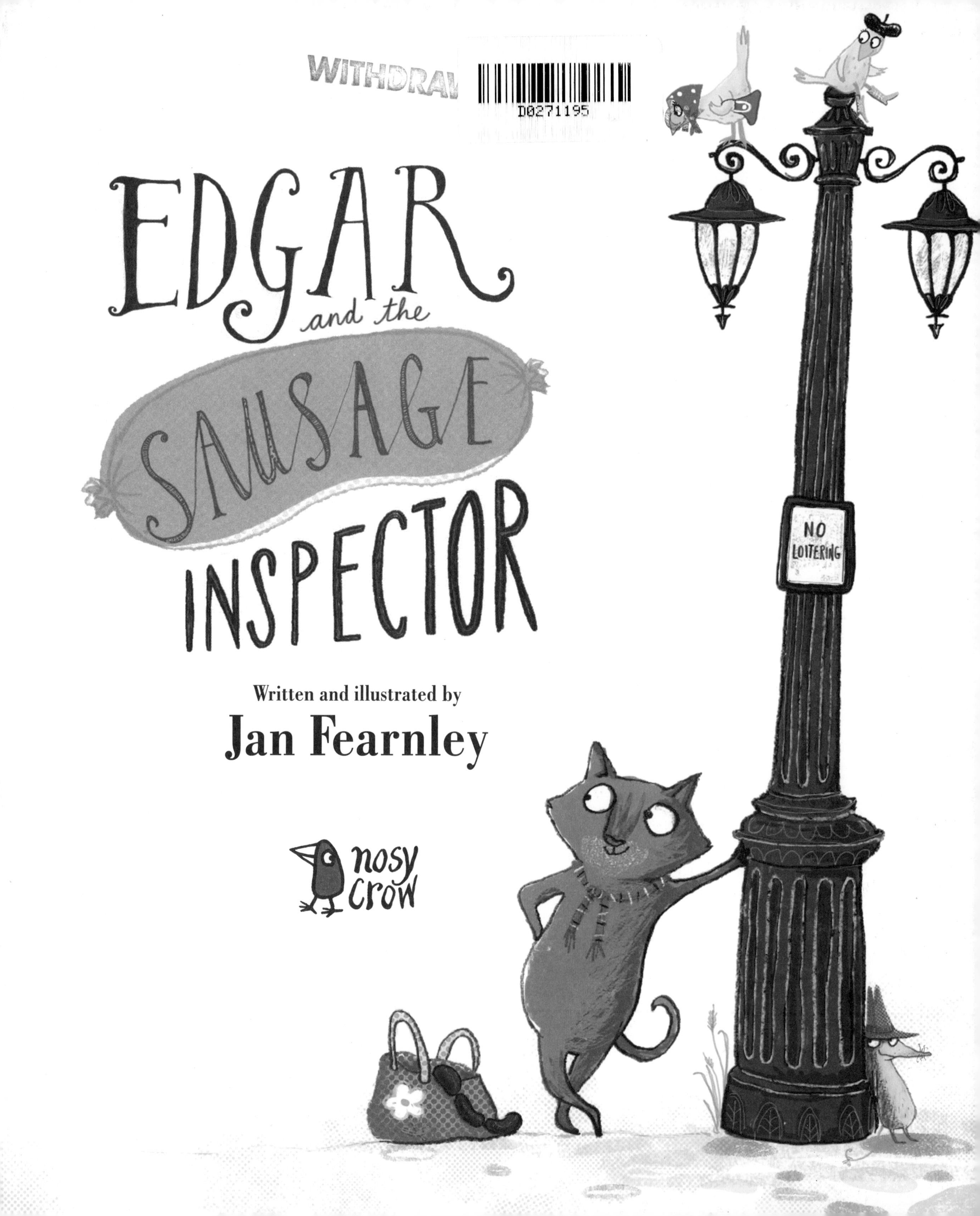
WITHDRAWN
D0271195
EDGAR
and the
SAUSAGE
INSPECTOR
Written and illustrated by
Jan Fearnley
nosy crow
NO
LOITERING

Edgar and his sister, **Edith,** lived in a funny little house at the end of a narrow little alley. Edgar loved Edith and tried to make her happy every day.

One day, Edith was feeling particularly hungry, so Edgar went to get something **special** for dinner.

CAT
ALLEY
À VENIR
BIENTÔT
L'Inspecteur
DES SAUCISSES

It wasn't long before he spotted
Edith's **favourite** thing – a nice string of sausages.
Edith **loved** sausages!

Edgar hurried home,
feeling **very** pleased with himself.
But then, a loud voice said . . .

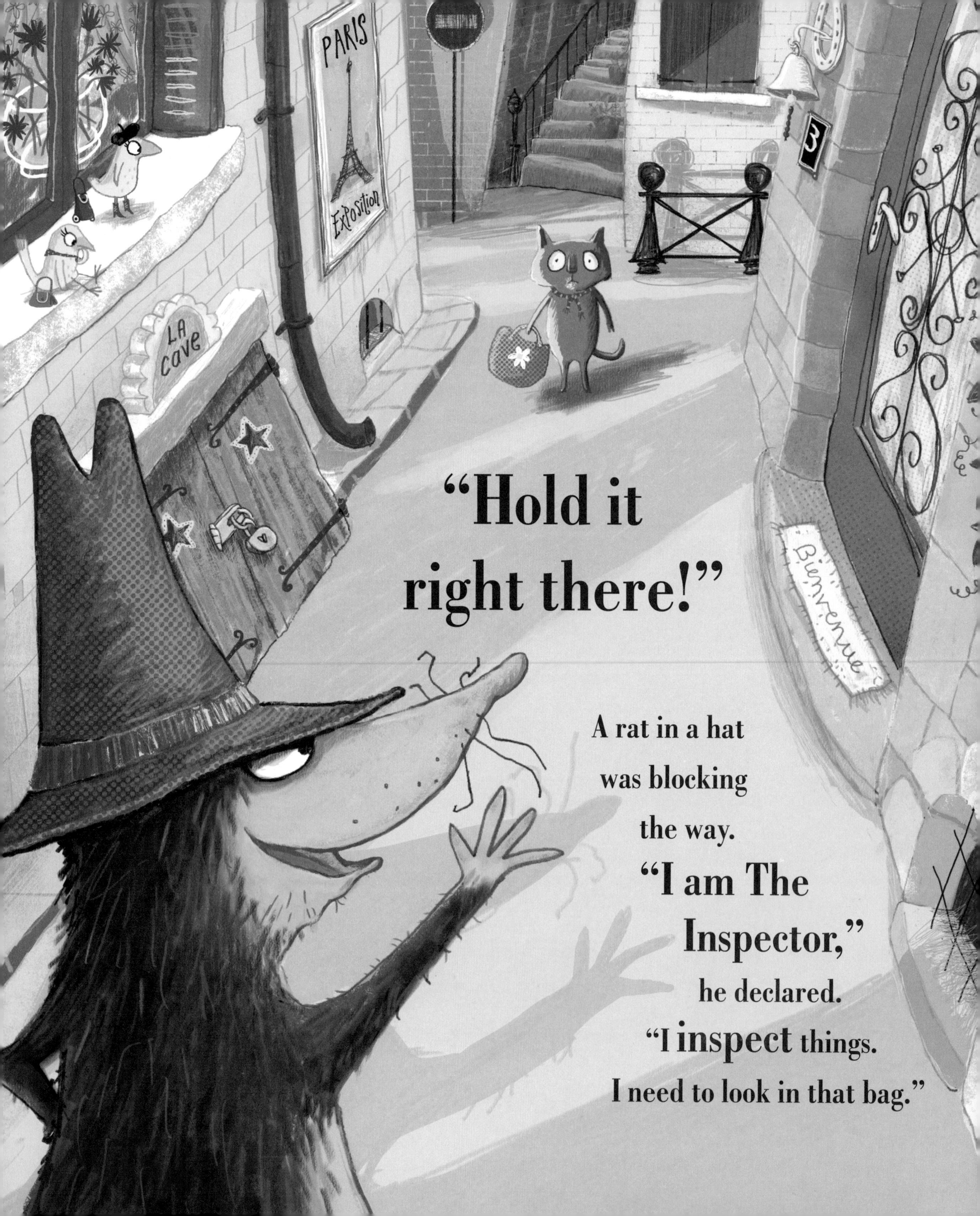

"Hold it right there!"

A rat in a hat was blocking the way.

"I am The Inspector," he declared.

"I **inspect** things. I need to look in that bag."

Edgar had never met **The Inspector** before.
The rat looked **very important.**
And he was wearing a **hat.**
So Edgar let The Inspector
look inside.

"Just as I suspected," he nodded. "**Bad** sausages.
I must take them away **at once** for further inspection."

The rat **snatched** the sausages and ran off,
squeeeeeeezing
through a hole in the wall.

Edgar and Edith had to make do with
dry crackers for dinner that night.
Edith could **hardly** believe it.

"You say a **rat** took our sausages?" she said.

"He looked **important,**" sighed Edgar.

"He was wearing a **hat.**"

The next day, Edgar decided to make up for losing the sausages with something **delightful** for Edith from the patisserie.

"She'll be **thrilled!**" he thought.

But when he turned back down the alley . . .

"Hold it right there!"

boomed a familiar voice. It was The Inspector again. This time, The Inspector had a hat and a badge. He looked very important – and decidedly plumper than before.

"I was right about the sausages," he said. "They were – mmm – bad."

"Are those **cakes?**" asked The Inspector.
"I've heard reports about **bad** cakes. I'd better **inspect** them. Hand them over."

"But they're **my** cakes," said Edgar.

"No complaining!" said The Inspector.
"I've got a **hat** and a **badge.** You'd better do as you're told!"

Edgar watched
miserably as
The Inspector **grabbed**
the cakes and
squeeeeeeezed
through a hole in the wall.

He trailed home with
empty paws.

Edith was not thrilled.
"That rat took our cakes, too?"
"He had a hat and a badge," said Edgar.

That night, Edith ate a jar of pickles.
Edgar had a limp stick of celery.
His tummy rumbled like a monster all night long.

The next day, Edith was **ravenous!**

She told Edgar she wanted

cakes . . .

sausages . . .

cheese . . .

ice cream . . .

and all sorts of **nice** things.

Edgar was **determined** to take home a **feast.**

His basket was heavy as he trundled down the alley. He **couldn't wait** to show Edith!

But . . .

Café
LIBRAIRIE PAPETERIE
LIBRAIRIE PAPETERIE
TABAC

"Hold it right there!"

The Inspector blocked the way. This time, he had a hat, a badge **and** a notebook, which rested against his **huge** belly. He looked **extremely important** – and **very** pleased with himself.

"I was **right** about the sausages.
I was **right** about the cakes.
They were – mmm-mmm – **bad.**"
He sniffed Edgar's basket, licked his lips
and put a **big** tick in his notebook.
"Just as I suspected. All this food is
very bad indeed . . .

It is my official duty to take it **all.**”
He **seized** the basket, and started
to pull it down the alley.

But Edgar had
had **enough.**

“Hold it . . .

. . . right there!”

shouted Edgar.

Edgar **snatched** the basket back,
sending everything **tumbling** to the ground.

The Inspector filled his paws
with whatever he could,
and made for the hole in the fence.

But that rat was now so **fat,**
he could hardly run!

"Stop!" yelled Edgar, chasing the **cheeky** little . . .
fat little . . . **juicy-looking** rat . . .

as he waddled rather
deliciously away.

Huffing and puffing, The Inspector tried to
squeeeeeeze himself through the hole in the fence.
But he was far too **fat** and far too **slow!**

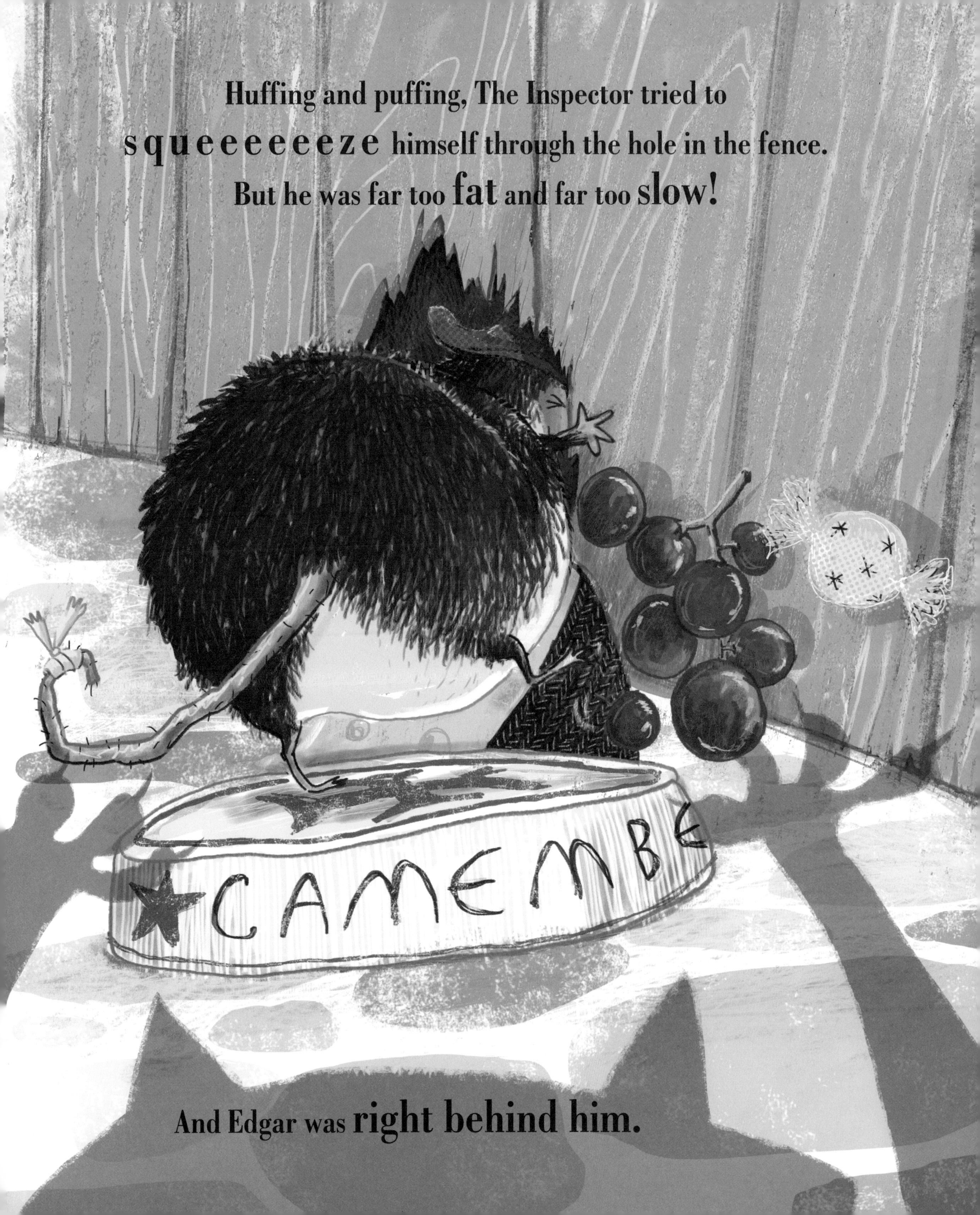

And Edgar was **right behind him.**

That evening, Edith dined like a queen.
"Oh, Edgar, you have **spoiled** me.
What a **delicious** feast!"

But Edgar **wasn't** hungry.

"Whatever is the matter?" asked Edith. "Where is your appetite? Have you been eating between meals?"

Edgar smiled a secret smile,
straightened his **hat** and polished his **badge.**
Then he put a **big** tick in his **notebook.**

"Yes, I did have a **cheeky** little something earlier," he smiled.
"It was very **fat** and **juicy,**
and, just as I suspected,
it was . . .

I AM the INSPEKTOR

. . . mmm-mmm-mmm – **bad!”**